First published in 2007 by
Franklin Watts
338 Euston Road
London
NW1 3BH

Franklin Watts Australia
Level 17/207 Kent Street
Sydney
NSW 2000

A CIP catalogue record for this book is available
from the British Library.

ISBN 978 0 7496 7082 5 (hbk)
ISBN 978 0 7496 7413 7 (pbk)

Series Editor: Melanie Palmer
Series Advisor: Dr Barrie Wade
Series Designer: Peter Scoulding

Printed in China

Franklin Watts is a division of
Hachette Children's Books.

HOPSCOTCH HISTORIES

Hoorah for
Mary
Seacole

by Trish Cooke and Anni Axworthy

W

FRANKLIN WATTS
LONDON•SYDNEY

About this book

Some of the characters in this book are made up,
but the subject is based on real events in history.
Mary Seacole (1805–1885) was born in Jamaica. She set
up her own hospital in Kingston Town to care for the
sick and wounded British soldiers. In 1854, when the
Crimean War broke out in Eastern Europe, British
soldiers joined the French and Turkish to battle against
the Russians. Mary decided to go to the Crimea to help.
She gave medicines to the injured soldiers and even went
out across the battlefield to treat them. When the war
ended in 1856, Mary settled in England. Her book about
her travels and adventures became a bestseller.

There was once a girl called Mary.
She lived on an island in the
Caribbean called Jamaica.

Mary's mother was a nurse.

She ran a hospital to look after

the British soldiers and sailors.

Mary's mother cooked for the soldiers and treated their illnesses.

Mary helped her mother make
medicines from the herbs and
plants in the garden.

"I want to be a nurse just like
you!" Mary said to her mother.

When Mary grew up she opened her own hospital. She wanted to be as good a nurse as her mother.

Mary used her own special herbs and plants to treat the soldiers. She became an excellent nurse.

The soldiers who stayed in Mary's hospital became her friends. "You're like a mother to us," they often said to her.

"Thank you, Mother Seacole,"
said a soldier called Thomas.
He became a good friend.

When a terrible disease called cholera spread in Jamaica, it made people very sick. Mary was quick to look after them.

One day, Mary heard there was a war in the Crimea. Many of her soldier friends went to fight there.

"I must go and help take care
of my soldiers," she said.
"Though it is a long way away!"

Mary sailed to the Crimea on a big ship called the "Hollander". The trip was long and the sea was rough.

Mary wasn't afraid of the big waves.
"Those poor soldiers need my help,"
she said bravely.

When she arrived, Mary went to the hospital in Scutari. There she met a nurse called Florence Nightingale.

Mary saw lots of injured soldiers and wanted to help them. But there was no room for her to stay.

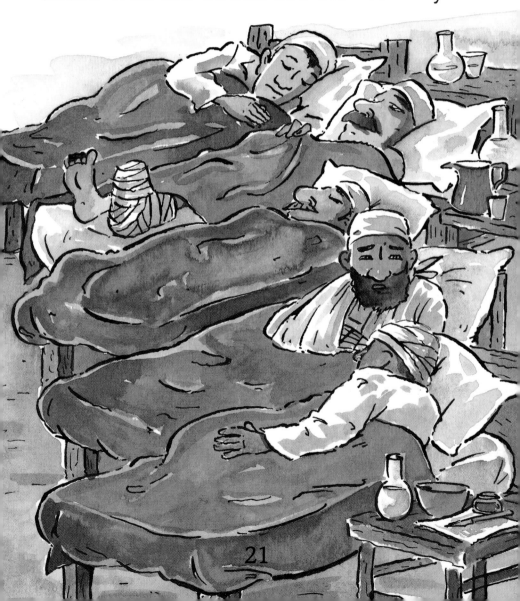

Mary decided to open her own
hospital in the Crimea instead.
"Hoorah! It's Mother Seacole!"
the soldiers cheered.

They remembered her from Jamaica
and looked forward to eating her
dinners. But Mary couldn't see her
friend Thomas anywhere.

Each day, Mary went out onto the battlefield to help the injured soldiers. She wasn't even afraid of the bullets that flew everywhere.

One day, she heard a voice call out:
"Mother Seacole!" She turned round
and saw an injured soldier.
She recognised him at once.

"Thomas!" she said. "It's you!"
Mary gave him some water and
helped with his injuries.

Then Mary brought Thomas back to her hospital. Before long he was well again.

"Hoorah for Mother Seacole!"
said Thomas. "Hoorah for Mother
Seacole!" the other soldiers shouted.

When the war ended, Mary went
to live in England. The soldiers held
a big concert to thank her for
making them better.

As Mary grew older, she decided to write a book about her life. Now we can all share her many adventures.

Hopscotch has been specially designed to fit the requirements of the National Literacy Strategy. It offers real books by top authors and illustrators for children developing their reading skills. There are 49 Hopscotch stories to choose from:

Marvin, the Blue Pig
ISBN 978 0 7496 4619 6

Plip and Plop
ISBN 978 0 7496 4620 2

The Queen's Dragon
ISBN 978 0 7496 4618 9

Flora McQuack
ISBN 978 0 7496 4621 9

Willie the Whale
ISBN 978 0 7496 4623 3

Naughty Nancy
ISBN 978 0 7496 4622 6

Run!
ISBN 978 0 7496 4705 6

The Playground Snake
ISBN 978 0 7496 4706 3

"Sausages!"
ISBN 978 0 7496 4707 0

The Truth about Hansel and Gretel
ISBN 978 0 7496 4708 7

Pippin's Big Jump
ISBN 978 0 7496 4710 0

Whose Birthday Is It?
ISBN 978 0 7496 4709 4

The Princess and the Frog
ISBN 978 0 7496 5129 9

Flynn Flies High
ISBN 978 0 7496 5130 5

Clever Cat
ISBN 978 0 7496 5131 2

Moo!
ISBN 978 0 7496 5332 3

Izzie's Idea
ISBN 978 0 7496 5334 7

Roly-poly Rice Ball
ISBN 978 0 7496 5333 0

I Can't Stand It!
ISBN 978 0 7496 5765 9

Cockerel's Big Egg
ISBN 978 0 7496 5767 3

How to Teach a Dragon Manners
ISBN 978 0 7496 5873 1

The Truth about those Billy Goats
ISBN 978 0 7496 5766 6

Marlowe's Mum and the Tree House
ISBN 978 0 7496 5874 8

Bear in Town
ISBN 978 0 7496 5875 5

The Best Den Ever
ISBN 978 0 7496 5876 2

ADVENTURE STORIES

Aladdin and the Lamp
ISBN 978 0 7496 6692 7

Blackbeard the Pirate
ISBN 978 0 7496 6690 3

George and the Dragon
ISBN 978 0 7496 6691 0

Jack the Giant-Killer
ISBN 978 0 7496 6693 4

TALES OF KING ARTHUR

1. The Sword in the Stone
ISBN 978 0 7496 6694 1

2. Arthur the King
ISBN 978 0 7496 6695 8

3. The Round Table
ISBN 978 0 7496 6697 2

4. Sir Lancelot and the Ice Castle
ISBN 978 0 7496 6698 9

TALES OF ROBIN HOOD

Robin and the Knight
ISBN 978 0 7496 6699 6

Robin and the Monk
ISBN 978 0 7496 6700 9

Robin and the Friar
ISBN 978 0 7496 6702 3

Robin and the Silver Arrow
ISBN 978 0 7496 6703 0

FAIRY TALES

The Emperor's New Clothes
ISBN 978 0 7496 7077 1 *
ISBN 978 0 7496 7421 2

Cinderella
ISBN 978 0 7496 7073 3 *
ISBN 978 0 7496 7417 5

Snow White
ISBN 978 0 7496 7074 0 *
ISBN 978 0 7496 7418 2

Jack and the Beanstalk
ISBN 978 0 7496 7078 8 *
ISBN 978 0 7496 7422 9

The Three Billy Goats Gruff
ISBN 978 0 7496 7076 4 *
ISBN 978 0 7496 7420 5

The Pied Piper of Hamelin
ISBN 978 0 7496 7075 7 *
ISBN 978 0 7496 7419 9

HISTORIES

Toby and the Great Fire of London
ISBN 978 0 7496 7079 5 *
ISBN 978 0 7496 7410 6

Pocahontas the Peacemaker
ISBN 978 0 7496 7080 1 *
ISBN 978 0 7496 7411 3

Grandma's Seaside Bloomers
ISBN 978 0 7496 7081 8 *
ISBN 978 0 7496 7412 0

Hoorah for Mary Seacole
ISBN 978 0 7496 7082 5 *
ISBN 978 0 7496 7413 7

Remember the 5th of November
ISBN 978 0 7496 7083 2 *
ISBN 978 0 7496 7414 4

Tutankhamun and the Golden Chariot
ISBN 978 0 7496 7084 9 *
ISBN 978 0 7496 7415 1

* hardback